15

0

Pl
on

To r
or

Y

For Amelie – my dancing star – the real Little Bird.
My parents who have given me endless support.
And every single-parent family that somehow makes it work. xxx
C.B.

For my wonderful Godmother, Aunty Ellen,
who never fails to make everyone smile.
Thank you for being such a fabulous person
and of course, my brilliant middle name! xxx
L.E.A.

First published in 2016 by Scholastic Children's Books
Euston House, 24 Eversholt Street
London NW1 1DB
a division of Scholastic Ltd
www.scholastic.co.uk
London – New York – Toronto – Sydney – Auckland
Mexico City – New Delhi – Hong Kong

Text copyright © 2016 Cerrie Burnell
Illustrations copyright © 2016 Laura Ellen Anderson

HB ISBN 978 1407 15221 9
PB ISBN 978 1407 15220 2

Ballet Dreams

Written by Cerrie Burnell

Illustrated by Laura Ellen Anderson

SCHOLASTIC

Once there was a girl who dreamed of dancing, of skipping over rooftops and pirouetting round the moon.

She could twirl on her toes as lightly as snow and dart through the air like a swallow.
So her Granddad called her...

...Little Bird.

One morning Little Bird's Mama woke her with a smile. "You can go and have a look at your new school today with Granddad."

"Oh I don't think I'll bother with school," Little Bird laughed, "I think I'll just do dancing."

Granddad chuckled and squeezed her hand, "Think of all the new things you'll learn: how to read books and spell your own name."

"But I want to be called **Little Bird** forever!" she sighed.

Then on the way to school,
Little Bird heard music and
she **tiptoed** through the doors
of a glittery old theatre.

There before her was a lake of
midnight swans, more beautiful
than anything Little Bird had ever seen.

"It's like watching a dream," she breathed. "It's the ballet of Swan Lake," said Granddad.

Through the air came a dancer with the lightness and grace of a dove. She was as elegant as nightfall, as dazzling as the moon.

"That's Odette, the swan princess!" said Granddad.

Little Bird was spellbound. She crept to the edge of the stage and murmured, "I want to fly like you."

Beneath the sparkling lights
the swan princess spoke,
"When you grow up you can join the
Midnight Swan Ballet company."

"But right now there's a **children's class** just starting –
would you like to join in?"

Little Bird's face lit up like a **star**.

Little Bird stepped into a room of long mirrors and children in pink satin shoes. Her feet felt lighter than feathers.

She **flitted** like a butterfly…

spun like an autumn leaf…

and **leaped** as high as a drifting cloud.

"Granddad, I don't need to go to school!"
Little Bird sang, "I need to go to **ballet!**"

"But even **ballerinas** go to school," smiled the swan princess and she pulled a snow-white **feather** from her crown.

"Everything you learn is like a feather," she whispered. "When you have gathered enough, they will spread out behind you like wings, and all that you've learned will help you to **fly**."

Little Bird held her feather
all the way to school.

"Oh Granddad," she cried, as
she skipped into a classroom
of **sunlight** and **stories**,
"I think I **will** like
it here after all."

"Just remember," grinned Granddad,
"Everything you learn will one day help you **fly**."

When Mama got home from the bakery, Little Bird flew into her arms. "I'm going to be a **ballerina**," she cried, "and my stage name will be... Little Bird!"

Mama giggled and together they held up the **feather** and wrote her name in the air.

Then Mama gazed at Little Bird's **expensive** new school bag. "Maybe you can start ballet next term," she said gently.

As Granddad listened he was still,
for he knew when Little Bird
danced, she shone, as if
her heart had brightened.

He stared at his golden watch.

And very quietly he went out.

The next morning, Little Bird
awoke to a wonderful surprise:
a pair of silken **ballet shoes!**

Mama gasped in amazement.

BALLERINAS
ONLY

Granddad smiled
his twinkly smile.
"You'll need them when
you start your lessons" he said.

When the first day of school came, Little Bird
was ready – she **danced** all the way there...

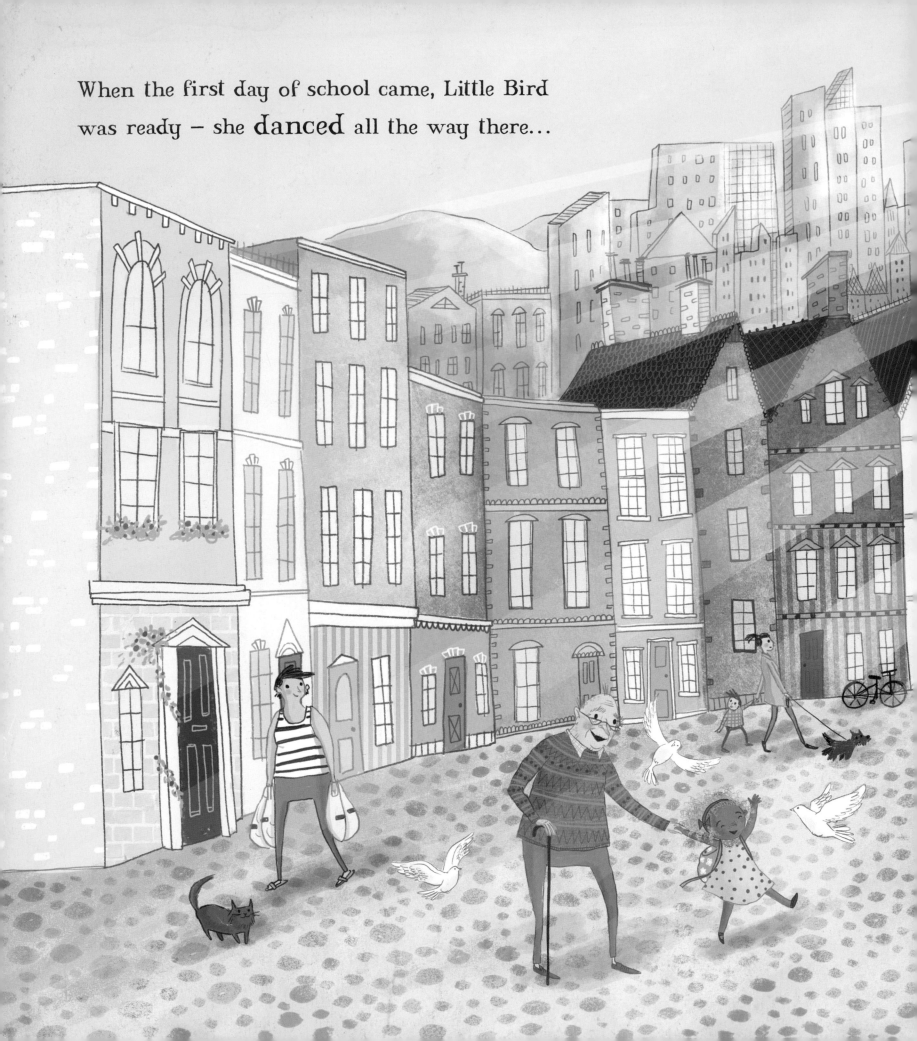

...and she danced all the way home
gathering **feathers** as she went.

In the end of term ballet show, Little Bird had a **starring** role!

Mama had given her a very special gift: a magnificent feather from a **real** midnight swan, so Little Bird would never forget her ballerina dream...

And one day
– just maybe –
she would be the
swan princess.